Tales of Tillie Terwillie
Who Does Tillie Love?

AUTHOR: MARY KAY LARSON

ILLUSTRATED BY: WENDI SUE LARSON

Graphic Designer: Debi Sue Root

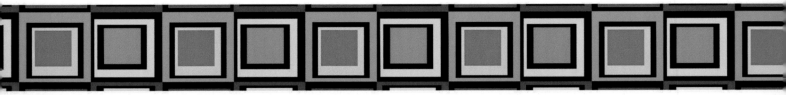

AuthorHouse™
1663 Liberty Drive
Bloomington, IN 47403
www.authorhouse.com
Phone: 833-262-8899

This book is printed on acid-free paper.

ISBN: 978-1-4772-6643-4 (sc)
ISBN: 979-8-8230-1234-8 (hc)
ISBN: 978-1-4772-7318-0 (e)

Print information available on the last page.

Published by AuthorHouse 07/24/2023

author**HOUSE**®

To the reader:

Theses stories are a simple way to help children identify and enjoy healthy relationships.

At the end of each story you will find one or two questions to engage your listener in some verbal interaction.

Enjoy!

INDEX

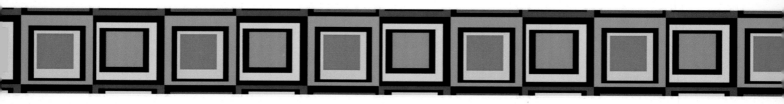

TILLLIE LOVES GREAT GRANDPA

There are things that Great Grandpa
can no longer do;

Like climbing high steps
and tying his shoes.

His legs are quite wobbly,
his cane he holds tight;

It's a fact that his **teeth** even
come out at night!

6

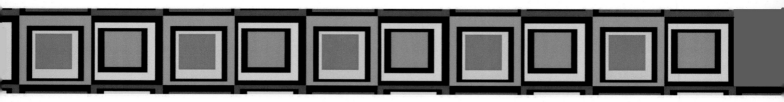

When he kisses his whiskers
tickle my cheek;

When he laughs he makes wheezes
and short little squeaks.

But mostly I like when he
takes time to *listen*;

Cause he *listens* and *listens*
and *listens* and *listens*.

I love my Great Grandpa;
I'll miss him I know;

When his visit is over and
it's his time to go.

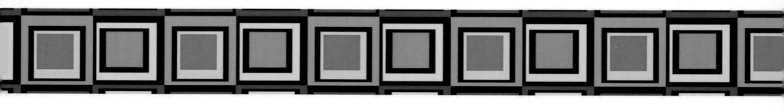

Here are some questions for you

Tillie's Great Grandpa is a good **listener.**

- Are you a good **listener**?

- Do you feel better when someone **listens** to you?

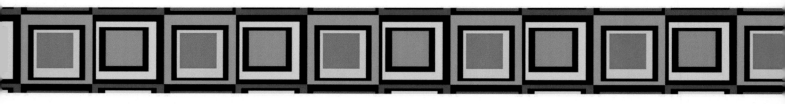

TILLIE LOVES HER FATHER

The *fishing* pole is mine,
it was given to me.

Just come to my house and
then you will see.

My dad is my partner,
we go to get bait.

We buy grubs and *great wigglies*
and head for the lake.

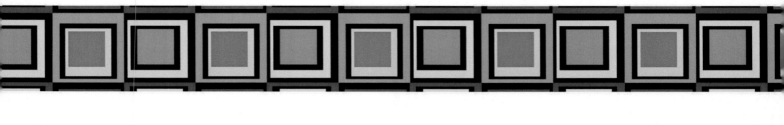

Daddy's Girl

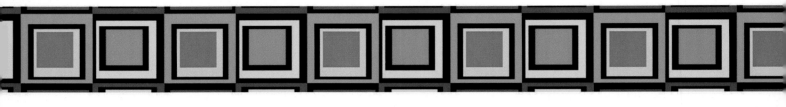

My hands get all icky and
my tennis shoes stink;

It's hard to remember
that they used to be *pink*.

It is worth it by far to go fishing with Dad;
It's the best time of summer a girl ever had!

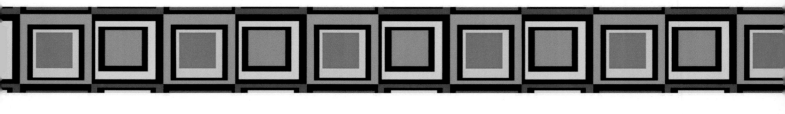

Here are some questions for you

- What favorite thing did you do last summer?

- Who did you do it with?

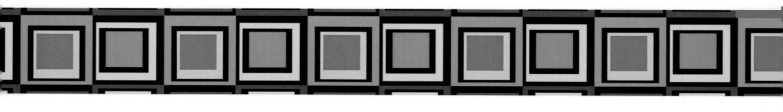

TILLIE LOVES HER FRIEND SADIE POTATIE

My *friend* Sadie Potatie lives on a big farm;

And when I am there we go in the red barn.

I walk in the dirt that the tractor just plowed.

I feed all the chickens and her
great big brown cow.

She shows me tree toads and
caterpillars and *lizards*;

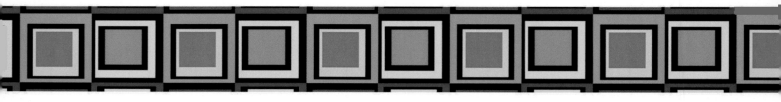

For lunch we eat apples and
chicken legs and *gizzards*.

When we're finished we go out and
play hide and seek;

Oh boy! I'm glad Sadie Potatie is
my *friend* for keeps!

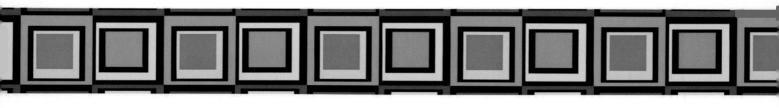

Here are some questions for you

- Can you find the **tree toad** and **frog** that live on Sadie's farm?

- How do **you** show someone that you want to be a good **friend**?

23

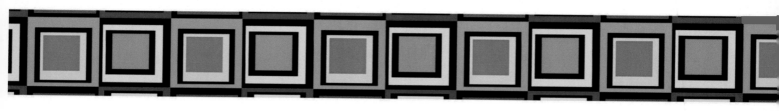

TILLIE LOVES HER AUNT NELLIE

What I love more than anything about
my Aunt Nellie;

Is the way that she dresses and her
perfume that's so smelly.

Her hats are so big
that the birds come to nest;

Her perfume is so **pleasurable**
it's impossible to resist.

25

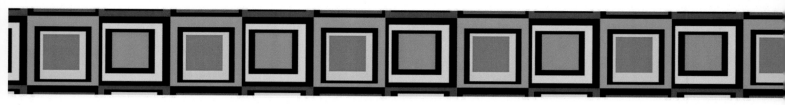

Her hair is all orange and
her cheeks are all red;

She puts on her roller skates and
jumps on my bed.

Can you see why I *love*
this Aunt Nellie of mine?

How excited I get because
there is never enough time;

To try all her hats and her perfume
that's so smelly.

Oh boy! I *love everything* about
my funny Aunt Nellie.

27

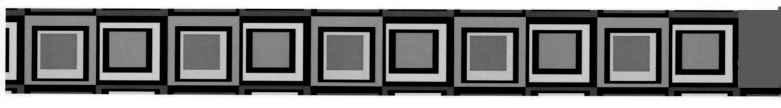

Here are some questions for you

- Do you know what **pleasurable** means?

- Can you see why Tillie **loves** her Aunt Nellie?

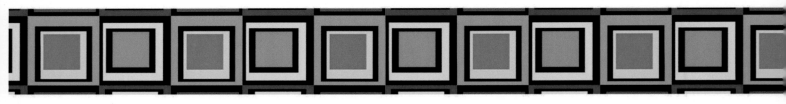

TILLIE LOVES HER BROTHER

Did you know that brothers like
all kinds of *gum*?

They like red gum and purple gum and
great wads of *bubble gum*.

They blow gigantic bubbles that
get stuck in their hair;

When they are naughty they get caught
putting it under their chair.

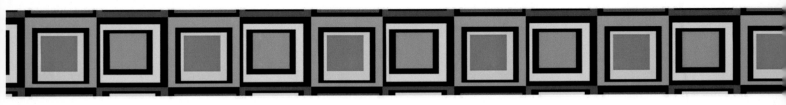

All this **gum** can get sticky and icky and bad;

It gets stuck on his **dog**
that looks silly and sad.

Sometimes when my brother drops it,
it gets stuck under his shoes;

And then my silly **brother**
does not know what to do.

Oh well—that's my brother who
gets all gooey and sticky;

Like **bubble gum** gets
when it gets him all icky!

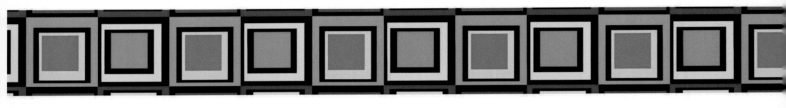

Here are some questions for you

- What should we do with our **gum** when we are finished chewing it?

  - Do you have a **silly** brother or a **silly** sister?

35

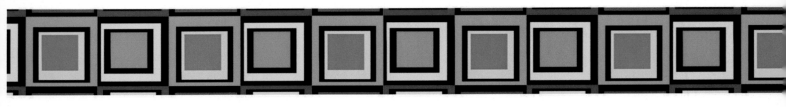

TILLIE LOVES HER
SISTER ANNIE BANANNIE

My sister Annie Bannanie fell on her *fanny*
while skating on the ice.

I helped her up but I fell on my *rump*
and that didn't feel very nice!

We giggled and wiggled until we were
standing and *wobbling* on our feet;

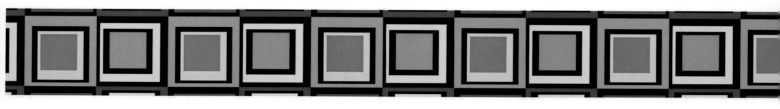

But low and behold in no time at all
we landed once more in a heap.

Annie Bannannie said her poor *fanny*
was definitely feeling quite *sore*;

And I said my *rump* was feeling the *bump* and
we should not skate any more!

39

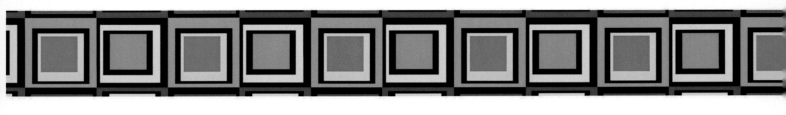

Here are some questions for you

- Did you ever fall on your **rump** and land with a **bump**?

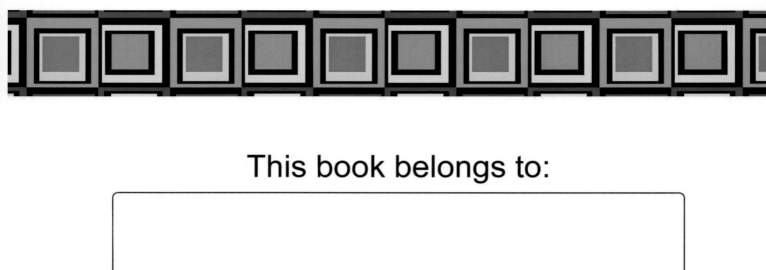

This book belongs to:

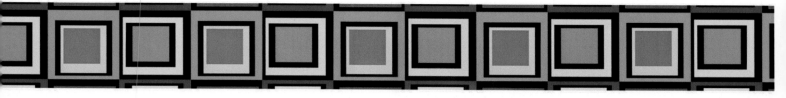

and I love…

Printed in the United States
by Baker & Taylor Publisher Services